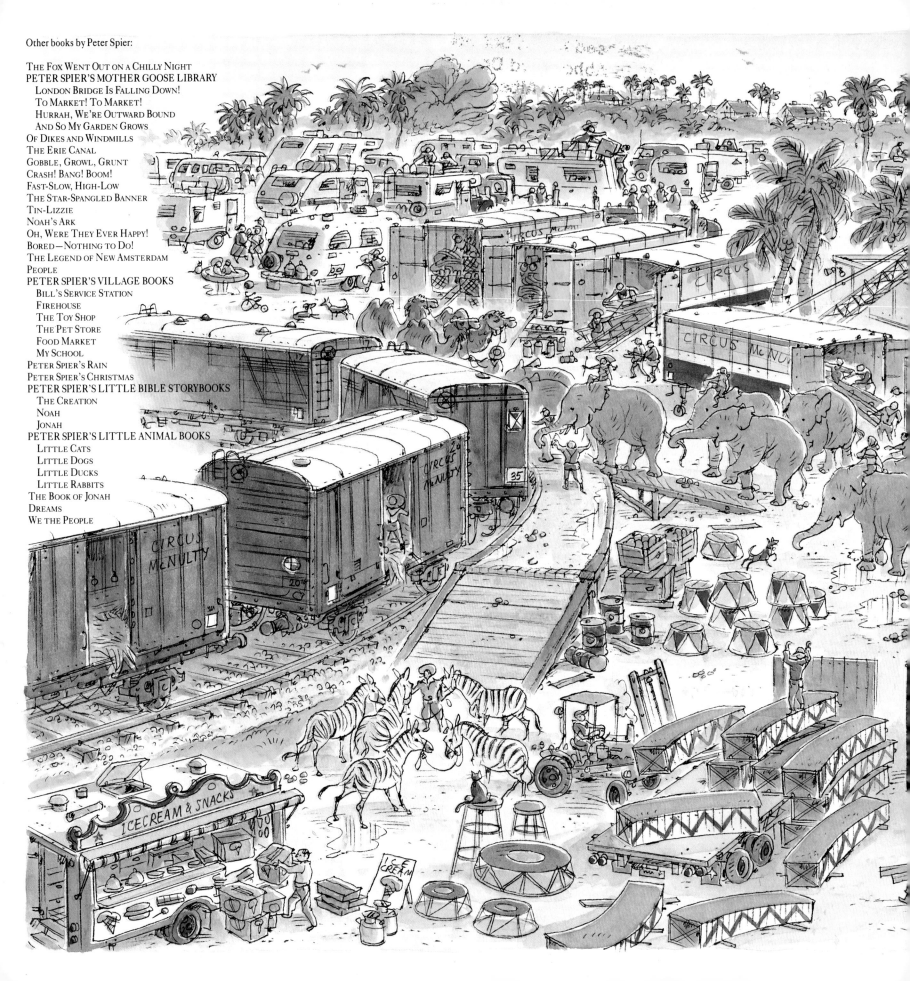

# Peter Spier's
# CIRCUS!

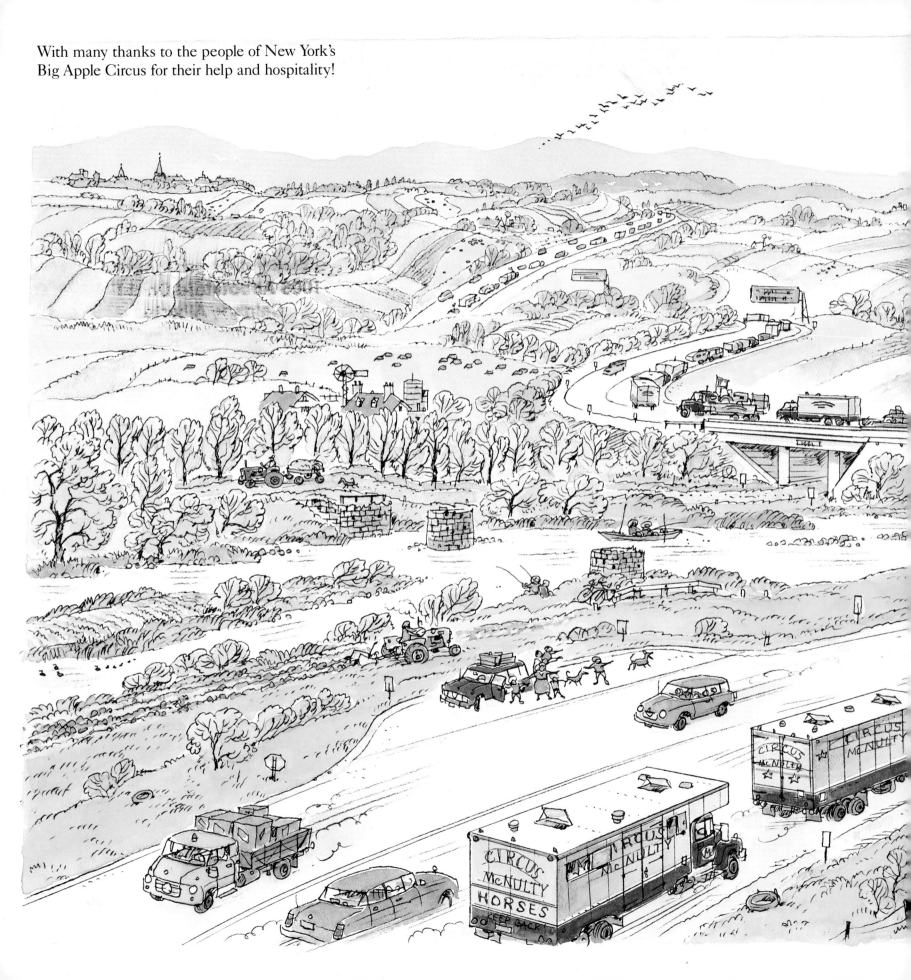

With many thanks to the people of New York's
Big Apple Circus for their help and hospitality!

# Peter Spier's
# C I R C U S !

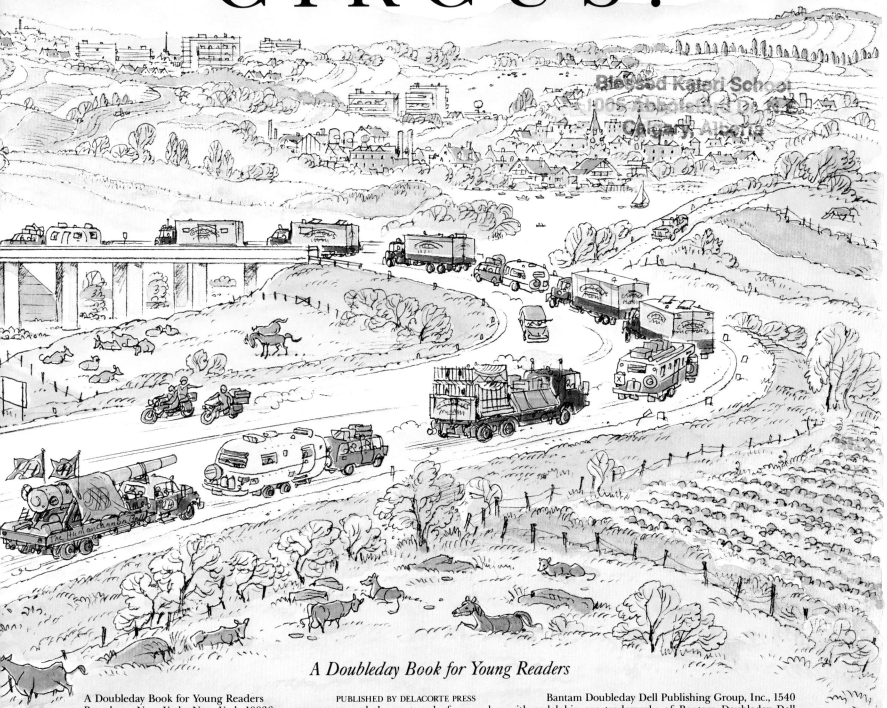

*A Doubleday Book for Young Readers*

A Doubleday Book for Young Readers    PUBLISHED BY DELACORTE PRESS    Bantam Doubleday Dell Publishing Group, Inc., 1540 Broadway, New York, New York 10036    DOUBLEDAY and the portrayal of an anchor with a dolphin are trademarks of Bantam Doubleday Dell Publishing Group, Inc.    Library of Congress Cataloging-in-Publication Data    Spier, Peter [Circus!] Peter Spier's circus! — 1st ed. p. cm.    Summary: A traveling circus arrives, sets up its village of tents, performs for the crowd, and then moves on again.    [1. Circus—Fiction.] I. Title. II. Title: Circus!    PZ7.S7544Cj 1991 [E]—dc20 90-23282 CIP AC    ISBN: 0-385-41969-4    Copyright © by Peter Spier
All rights Reserved    Printed in the United States of America    October 1992    First Edition    7 6 5 4 3

Setting up: a crew of 32 men and women. Riggers, mechanics, carpenters, plumbers, and electricians...

...14 acres of canvas...100 miles of ropes and wires...telephone lines...7 miles of electrical cables...2,200 seats...stables, a commissary, and workshops...and all that in just under 12 hours!

The instant circus village. Everyone is here now. Except the elephants. They're coming by train tonight.

The circus veterinarian, Dr. Hofmeyer, checks out each animal carefully after their long journey. Caesar, a horse, is not feeling well. "No work for him tomorrow," says the vet, "just let him rest." And Bessie in the next stall is expecting any day now. She gets a whole month off!

The circus laundry and grocery—on wheels.

Feeding time. 250 pounds of fish, tons of hay and grains, meat, bananas, apples, carrots, and fresh fruit. Not to mention the cans of dog food, wood chips and straw for bedding, and lots and lots of water.

2 A.M.

Mr. McNulty, the owner, manager, and ringmaster, in his office trailer. Mrs. McNulty is paying bills, salaries, insurance policies, feed bills, and much, much more.

This is where the Laszlos live. They are Hungarian jugglers from Budapest.

Mr. Uzelli from Naples, Italy, is one of the clowns. His wife sells tickets.

The Hozumis in their trailer with Yoko and Tamo. He is an acrobat. Mrs. Hozumi stays home to teach their children, for they speak only Japanese.

Some of Yoko's homework.

The Wilkinsons are from New Zealand. He is the chief electrician, and she sells programs.

The Dijkstras from Holland own six poodles. Pretty crowded motor home.

This is the circus school. Six grades, and Mrs. Knapp teaches them all in a trailer. The older children go to school at home. Mr. Knapp drives the tractor-trailer and is also a stilt walker.

Mr. Knapp.

Rehearsing! The first performance will be at eight tonight.

The legendary Henriquez Family on the high wire:

mother, father, three sons, one daughter, and one son-in-law. They come from Spain.

Mario Uzelli and his Polish partner, Felek Wisniewski, putting on their makeup.

Everybody else is getting into their costumes as well.

Wow! Some change.

Only twenty minutes to showtime now . . .

After having welcomed everyone, the ringmaster, Mr. McNulty, says,
"And now, ladies and gentlemen, we will start with the GREAT PARADE!"

Sarah Cunningham is a trick rider. Her husband George's act comes later.
She's Australian and he's British.

Hey, here is the horse act of Uzelli and Wisniewski. Kind of funny.

These acrobats came all the way from Japan.

Ivan the Russian Bear on his bike, with his trainer, Vladimir Smirnoff. He's Russian too.

Those seals are just as good at catching fish as at balancing balls on their snouts. Oh, and throwing the fish is Wencke Dahl from Norway.

Mr. and Mrs. Hans Schlossberg from Germany, and their six Indian elephants, Pathan, Hindu, Jhoola, Gurka, Sikh, and Gretchen (Gretchen...? Funny name for an Indian elephant).

Big elephants sometimes leave a big mess...

Plate spinning is an ancient Chinese art, and these performers
are from Beijing, China.

George Cunningham and his wonderfully trained horses. There should have been twelve, but remember Caesar and Bessie? By the way, Caesar is feeling much better today.

And here we have the McNultys' son Sean and his hippopotamus. Standing on that barrel is all the hippo can do, but that's pretty good for a hippo. And guess who are making fun of Sean and his hippo?

I bet you have never seen a springboard act like this one. They're Turks.

Jack Harris, "the Human Cannonball" (he's from Peoria, Illinois), sliding into the muzzle of his cannon.

The gun barrel is elevated to the exact angle...

. . . and with a loud bang, and a cloud of smoke, Jack is shot a hundred feet by compressed air into the safety net. Pretty daring!

Not many people could equal this. But the Mirabeaus know how to, and like so many circus acts, they are all related. They hail from France.

"Ladies and gentlemen!" bellows Mr. McNulty. "It is intermission time. You can stretch your legs for half an hour, buy refreshments, and visit our stables."

During the intermission a great iron cage is set up, with a strong net over it.

This is always an exciting moment. Mr. and Mrs. Gaston Vermeylen from Belgium are the owners and trainers. Looks dangerous—and it is.

Why is that small car driving into the ring?

Look at the Garcias from Mexico. Just imagine the strength this must take.

Austrian Mr. Bauer takes a bow with his llamas. They have more hair than he does!

So that's why! How did they ever manage to pack eleven people and a dog into a car that small? It must have been pretty tight inside.

The Dijkstras' poodles are great at jumping and pushing. That dog in the baby carriage has an easy job. But they all take turns at it.

The French trapeze artists are tensely waiting and warming up. They are the world-renowned Pelletiers. And some act it is.

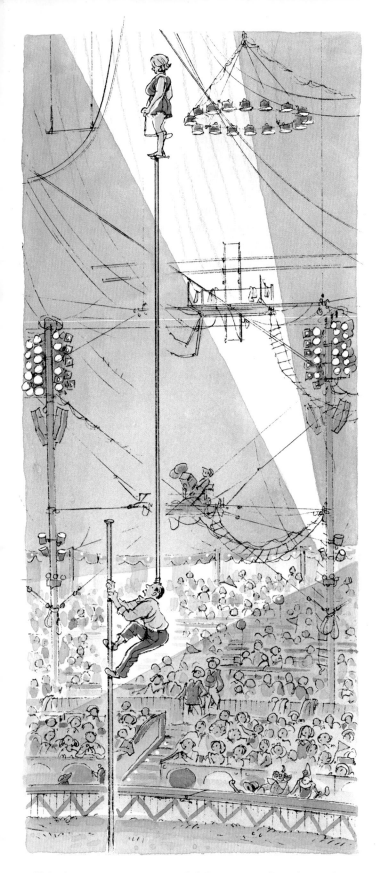

Look at the chimps Mathilda and Reggie balancing on their poles—and in their best clothes, too. Kathy MacDonald from Canada is their trainer.

Right now you could hear a pin drop in the tent. The Hudsons are truly fantastic with their perch-pole routine.

And guess who are aping whom?

Many people will tell you that Lippizaners are the most beautiful horses on earth. But all good things must come to an end...

The horses get a big hand...

...so does the band...

...and Mr. McNulty thanks everyone for coming, and wishes them a good night before the Grand Finale.

It is all over for tonight...

. . . but not for the cleanup crew!

Dawn. Time to move on. The elephants are on their way back to the train, the performers are driving off, and in six hours there will not be a trace left of the circus...